D1437010

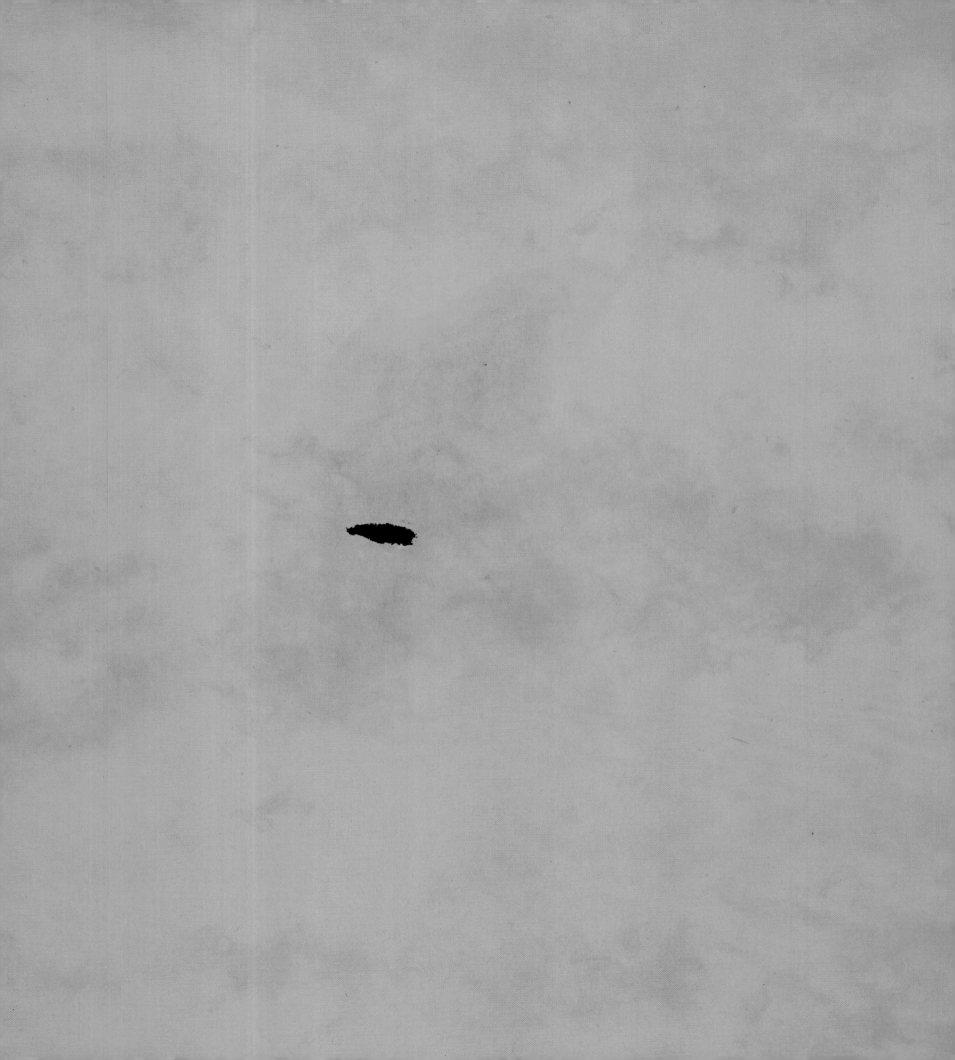

BIG MAMA MAKES THE WORLD

For Amy with love ✦ P.R.

To Hattie ✦ H.O.

First published 2002 by Walker Books Ltd
87 Vauxhall Walk, London SE11 5HJ

10 9 8 7 6 5 4 3 2 1

Text © 2002 Phyllis Root
Illustrations © 2002 Helen Oxenbury

The right of Phyllis Root and Helen Oxenbury to be identified
as author and illustrator respectively of this work has been asserted
by them in accordance with the Copyright, Designs and Patents Act 1988

This book has been typeset in StonePrint and Aquinas.

Printed in Italy

All rights reserved

British Library Cataloguing in Publication Data:
a catalogue record for this book is available
from the British Library

ISBN 0-7445-7382-3

HAMPSHIRE COUNTY LIBRARY	
1861568	
Peters	05-Dec-02
JF	£12.99
0744573823	

BIG MAMA
MAKES THE
WORLD

Written by Phyllis Root

Illustrated by Helen Oxenbury

WALKER BOOKS
AND SUBSIDIARIES
LONDON · BOSTON · SYDNEY

When Big Mama made the world,
she didn't mess about.

There was water, water everywhere,
and Big Mama saw
what needed to be done.
She rolled up her sleeves and went to it.
It wasn't easy, either,
with that little baby on her hip.

But nothing stops Big Mama.
Not for a second.

"Light," said Big Mama,
and – would you believe it? –
there was light.

"Dark," said Big Mama,
and there was the dark,
as big as the light.

"You two have work to do,"
Big Mama said.
"And no fooling around."

Then Big Mama looked
        at the light and the dark,
        and she looked at that little baby
        looking at the light and the dark,
        smiling and gurgling,
        and she said,
        "Good. That's very, very good."

        And that's how the first day went by.

The next day, Big Mama looked around.
"I can't tell my up from my down," she said.
"We better have some sky here."

And there it was, the big sky,
    wrapping round everything
    and as soft and blue as a baby's blanket.
There wasn't much else yet,
    but the water and the light,
    the dark and the sky were all doing
    what Big Mama wanted them to
    and she was pleased.
"Good," she said. "That's very, very good."

That's how the second day went by.

The next day, Big Mama
        looked around again and said,
        "We've got light
        and we've got dark,
        but I still can't tell what time of day it is.
How am I going to know when it's morning,
        or evening, or time to put the baby
        down for a nap?"

What Big Mama wants,
        Big Mama gets. That's how it is.

"Sun," said Big Mama.
"You take care of this day business for me."

"Moon," said Big Mama.
"You take care of the night."

Big Mama made the stars too,
in case the moon ever overslept.

Then she looked at the sun and moon
and stars filling up her sky,
just in time for the little baby's nap,
and she nodded
and smiled
and said,
"Good. That's very, very good."

That's how the third day went by.

The next morning, Big Mama got up
with the sun and said,
"We need a place to put our feet down
when they need putting down."
She knew there'd be some feet-putting-down soon –
that baby of hers was growing every day.

"Earth," said Big Mama. "Come here."
And it did.

A big ball of mud it was –
not much to look at.
Baby liked it just the way it was,
but Big Mama had hardly even started.

"I need some grass to wriggle my toes in,"
    said Big Mama.
"And some old shady trees to hang a hammock in.
And some papayas and oranges and plums to eat."

So it was. Just like she said.
Little baby sucked on a mango
    and there were grass and trees and fruit
    all over the place,
    as if someone had tipped up a fruit stall.

Big Mama looked at the earth and said,
    "Good. That's very, very good."

That's how the fourth day went by.

Most people would have been happy
    to leave it at that, but Big Mama
    doesn't call a job done till it's finished
    and finished properly.

Big Mama looked at
    the water and earth
    and trees and sky and sun
    and moon and stars, and she said,
    "It's too quiet down there.
We better have some whales
    and some birds
    and some fish."

So, of course, that's exactly what happened.

Soon there were more whales and
        minnows and parrots and crows
        than a little baby could shake a stick at
        (which a little baby could do,
        if a little baby wanted to,
        now that Big Mama had made
        the trees full of sticks).

Big Mama looked at all the commotion and said,
        "Good. That's very, very good."

That's how the fifth day went by.

Big Mama had nearly had enough.
Making a world was a lot of work, what with the
laundry piling up and the plates needing washing.

She thought she'd finish things off in one big bang.
"I need some creepers and crawlers," she said.
"Some runners and jumpers.
Some diggers and divers.
And anyone else who wants to be created –
now's your chance!"

Hedgehogs and lizards, otters
and snakes, rabbits and polar bears –
that's how Big Mama made them all.

One Big Bang !

But she hadn't finished yet. Oh no.

"I'm lonely," said Big Mama.
"Who's going to sit on the step
    and tell stories with me?
Not you creepers and crawlers.
Not you diggers and divers.
You're good friends,
    but none of you can tell a story.
And all this little baby can say so far is,
    'goo-goo-ga-ga'.
I need some people to keep me company."

So Big Mama
        scooped up some leftover mud
        and she pushed and pulled
        and she poked and pried,
        and – the next thing you know –
        there were people everywhere.

Big people and little people.
Fat people and thin people.
All sorts of shades of people.

And every one of them
        had a story to tell Big Mama.

"Good," said Big Mama.
        "That's very, very good."

That's how the sixth day went by,
	with Big Mama and all the people
	sitting on the step laughing and talking,
	while the sun went down.

Big Mama was ready for a rest now,
        ready to curl up with that little baby of hers
        in the big blue blanket of sky.
But she had one more thing to do.

She lined up all the people and said,
"This is a fine world we've got here
        and you better take good care of it.
I'm taking a day off now,
        but I'll be keeping an eye on you."

That's what she said.
And she meant it.

And every now and then,
   when she's burping the baby
   or baking biscuits,
Big Mama looks down
   and says,
   "You better straighten up down there."

And every now and then, she looks down
     on this beautiful little world she's made,
     and she nods
     and smiles
     and says,

"Good. That's very, very good."